Published by Frog, Ltd.

Frog, Ltd. books are distributed by
North Atlantic Books
P.O. Box 12327
Berkeley, California 94712

Cover and book design by Paula Morrison

Printed in Singapore
Distributed to the book trade by Publishers Group West

North Atlantic Books' publications are available through most bookstores. For further information, call 800-337-2665 or visit our website at www.northatlanticbooks.com.

Substantial discounts on bulk quantities are available to corporations, professional associations, and other organizations. For details and discount information, contact our special sales department.

Library of Congress Cataloging-in-Publication Data

Jones, Andrea, 1969–
    The spitting twins / by Andrea Jones ; illustrations by Joe Kulka.
    p. cm.
    Summary: When nine-year-old twins Andy and Zach break their school's no-spitting rule, their teacher tries to identify them as other spitting creatures, such as llamas, clams, and fruit bats, before explaining why they should not spit.
    ISBN 1-58394-095-2 (cloth)
    [1. Behavior—Fiction. 2. Schools—Fiction. 3. Animals—Habits and behavior—Fiction.] I. Kulka, Joe, ill. II. Title.
    PZ7.J6814Sp 2004
    [E]—dc22
                                                    2004014296

          1 2 3 4 5 6 7 8 9 TWP 09 08 07 06 05 04

The Spitting Twins

Andrea Jones

illustrated by

Joe Kulka

Frog, Ltd.
Berkeley, California

One day at school, Andy and Zach broke the ABSOLUTELY NO SPITTING rule.

They spit at the girls as they came off the slide, and the boys as they soared on the swings.

They even spit on each other, which was very awful—because they were brothers.

Their teacher, Mrs. Gedrose, caught them spitting.
She hustled them off the playground.

She sat them down in her classroom, quick as a wink and on the double.

The boys thought they were in for it, but Mrs. Gedrose didn't yell or scold or even stand them in a corner. She only asked, "Why are you boys spitting? I can't think of one good reason why a boy should spit."

The twins shrugged.

Why, indeed?

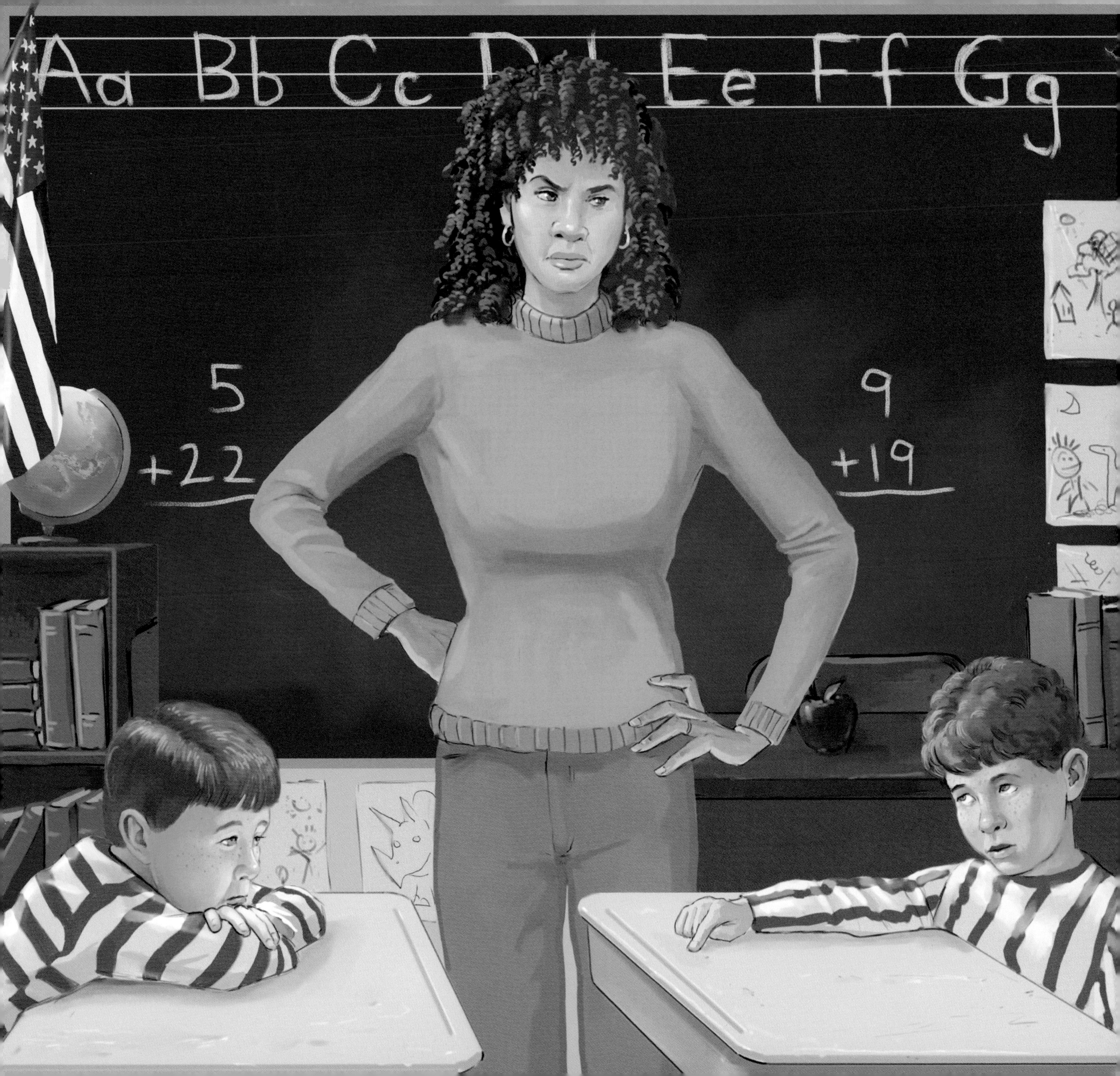
Aa Bb Cc
Ee Ff Gg
5
+22
9
+19

"You know, maybe you're not boys at all. You might possibly be furry llamas. They spit slimy goo at anyone who bothers them when they're upset."

"Gross!" said Zach and Andy. "We're not llamas! That's not why we spit."

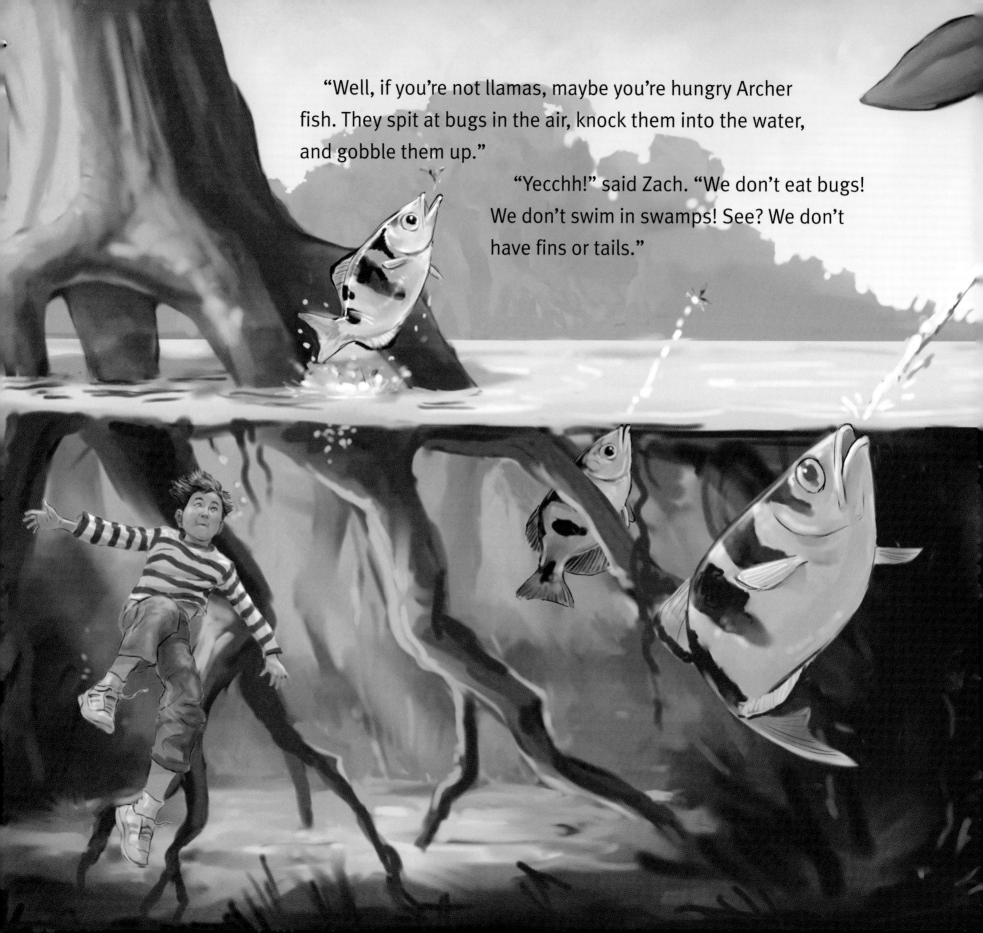

"Well, if you're not llamas, maybe you're hungry Archer fish. They spit at bugs in the air, knock them into the water, and gobble them up."

"Yecchh!" said Zach. "We don't eat bugs! We don't swim in swamps! See? We don't have fins or tails."

"Aha, I've got it. I think I've caught two really big clams!" She nodded with certainty. "You MUST be clams! They dig in the sand, and suck in water filled with food. They eat the food and spit out the water. When you stand on the beach, you can see them squirting."

"We don't live underneath the sand," Andy protested, tiredly.
"We're kids. We live in a regular house."

Mrs. Gedrose got up and paced around the room, staring at the boys. "Hmm. It's true, I don't see any clam shells on you. I doubt you're clams."

She paused in front of a picture on her bulletin board. Then she smiled mischievously and turned slowly to the twins. "You know, I've got it. You're CAMELS!"

"Camels spit when they're fighting. Hmmm—
I think I see humps on your back . . . and is that
a CAMEL TAIL?"

Zach and Andy jumped from their chairs and felt their seats for tails. They were relieved to find just the pockets of their pants.

"We don't have camel tails," Zach said with relief. "And our backs don't have humps."

"We'll never spit again, Mrs. Gedrose," said Andy. "We promise."

"I'm not convinced," Mrs. Gedrose said. "I need to be quite certain. There's another creature who spits ..."

"Might you be furry Fruit
Bats? They spit out seeds while they
eat fruit—a messy situation when
you're hanging by your feet!"

Mrs. Gedrose wrinkled her brow with
worry. "Dear me," she said. "I'd rather
you were one of *these* spitting animals
and not … the kind that spits acid."

"Where—are those?" they gasped.

"Up in the woods where the pine trees grow, there's a millipede who lives in the dirt. He's long and brown and mostly stays hidden. But if you bother him, he'll squirt you with acid to protect himself. It's very painful."

Zach and Andy shuddered at the vision of this creepy bug.

"We're not millipedes, are we Zach," said Andy, looking at his brother.

"No, Andy. I'm sure we don't spit acid."

Mrs. Gedrose walked around her desk and touched their skin. "You know, I do believe your skin is getting ever so slightly scaly. Could it be? Are you sure you're not one of those cobras that Indian snake charmers coax out of baskets?"

"Andy, we should tell her," said Zach.

"OK," said Andy in a small voice. He cleared his throat and summoned up his courage. "We love *ballplayers,* Mrs. Gedrose. Especially pitchers. They spit on their gloves! They spit chewing tobacco before they pitch. They look *so* cool."

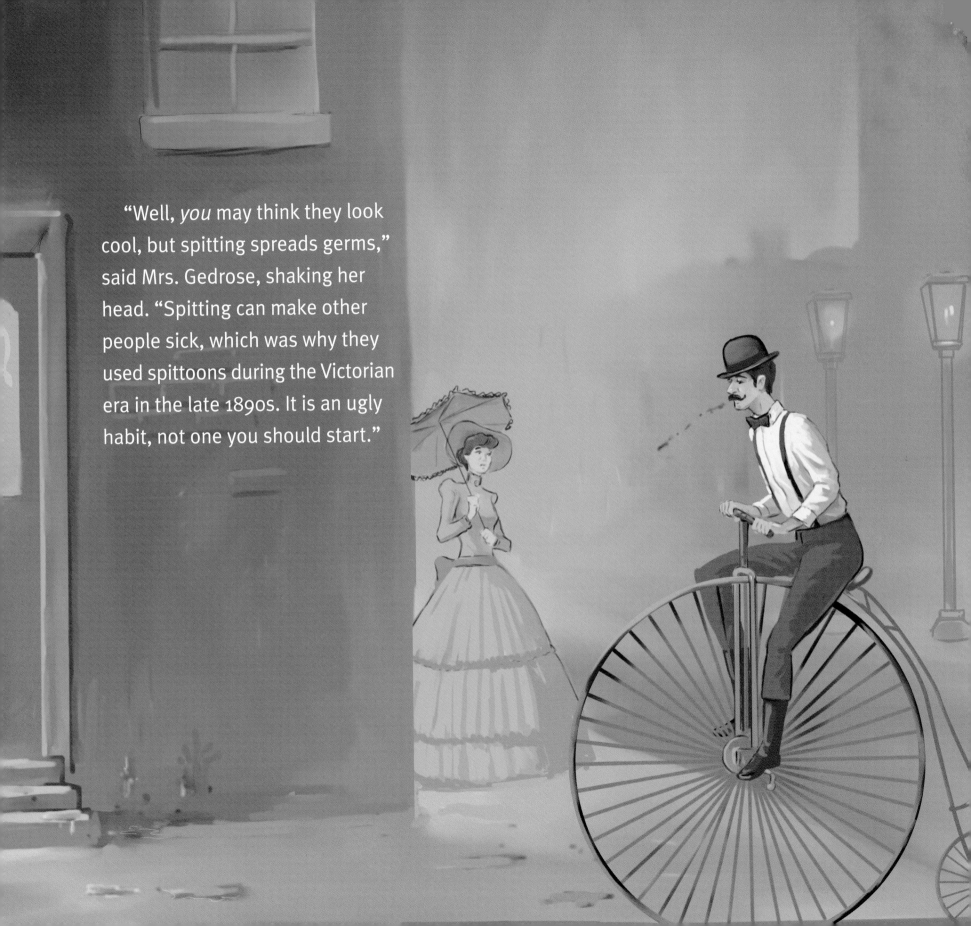

"Well, *you* may think they look cool, but spitting spreads germs," said Mrs. Gedrose, shaking her head. "Spitting can make other people sick, which was why they used spittoons during the Victorian era in the late 1890s. It is an ugly habit, not one you should start."

Andy and Zach looked at each other. They shook their heads. "We don't want to spit tobacco," said Zach. "We just like to see everyone screaming and running away. Especially the girls!"

"Andy, Zach—" said Mrs. Gedrose. "Humans don't spit at others—it's a nasty thing to do. It shows disrespect for another person. And we can't have wild animals creating pandemonium in our school."

Mrs. Gedrose's eyes twinkled. "When is the one time it's OK to spit?" She took something from her desk and held it behind her back.

Andy and Zach thought a moment. "I know!" yelled Zach.

"When you're brushing your teeth with toothpaste, of course!"

"But not at each other," said Andy.

"I think you've got it, " said Mrs. Gedrose, handing them new toothbrushes. "Now, run along and play with your friends."

And the twins never, ever, spit at anyone again.

About the Animals

 Llamas are among the oldest domestic animals in the world. Their foot is a leathery pad with two toenails, which makes them sure-footed. They are used as pack animals in South America. Llamas have a calm disposition, but a bad reputation for spitting at other llamas when fighting over food.

 The Archer fish can shoot a jet of water out of its mouth as many as seven times in a row, to knock down flying bugs or those walking on plants above. It can leap up to 12 inches out of the water and catch bugs in its mouth.

 Clams live from the high-tide line to very deep parts of the ocean. They are well built for digging and eating, with a muscular foot for digging. Once the clam has dug into the sand, it sucks in water filled with food particles, which it eats, then spits out the rest. You can see some clams spitting up through the sand.

 Millipedes live near the surface of the dirt and eat old plants. If some varieties of millipedes are scared, they will curl up into a tight spiral, and only "spit" their acid if whatever is scaring them won't go away.

 Dromedary Camels have only one hump, but they don't store water there. Desert people use camels for packing and riding in the desert. The camel protects itself from flying sand with very long eyelashes and nostrils that can be closed. The camel can drink up to 30 gallons of water in just 10 minutes, and spits when it gets angry at other camels or people.

 Fruit bats have long, webbed fingers that serve as wings. They aren't blind, but have a keen sense of smell and sight. They hang upside down during the day and fly at night, foraging for food. To land, they crash into bushes or trees, or grab a branch as they fly by. Fruit bats suck on fruit and flowers, swallowing the nectar and spitting out pulp and seeds.

 When the Indian Spitting Cobra is scared of a human or animal, it will rise up and spread its hood. Stay away! It spits its venom into the eyes of its predators and blinds them. The Indian Cobra eats mice, lizards, and frogs, and like all snakes, swallows its dinner whole. The Indian Cobra guards her eggs for about 50 days until they hatch.